BONGO LARRY

Daniel Pinkwater

Illustrated by Jill Pinkwater

MARSHALL CAVENDISH • NEW YORK

"HELLO,"

I said. "This is Martin Frobisher, owner of the Hotel Larry."

"Hello," a voice said. "This is the police."

"What is wrong?" I asked.

"We have your bear. He was making a disturbance with some other bears."

"He is not my bear. He is my friend. My hotel, the Hotel Larry, is named after him."

"He was playing a drum in the public park at night," the policeman said.

I heard Larry's voice saying, "Not a drum. They are bongos. I was playing bongos, man."

"We have your bear," said the policeman.

"I will be right there," I said.

At the police station, I had to sign a paper saying I promised that Larry would not make noise at night.

"It was not noise. It was music," Larry said.

"Who are the bears he was with, and where are they?" I asked the policeman.

"He was with three other bears, Bear Number One, Bear Number Three, and a bear named Roy—all polar bears."

"Roy is his brother," I said.

"All three bears gave their address as the City Zoo," the policeman said. "The zoo sent a taxi for them."

"I am sure the bears meant no harm," I told the policeman.

"It is against the law for bears to make noise in the park after eight o'clock," the policeman said. "If they do it again, someone will have to pay a fine."

"I am sure Larry understands," I said.

"Policemen are squares," Larry said.

In the car, I said, "Larry, I am surprised at you. I do not mind that you bongoed in the park after eight o'clock, but it was rude for you to say that policemen are squares. They are only doing their job."

"Well, I am rebelling," Larry said.

"You are rebelling? What are you rebelling against?"

"What have you got?" Larry asked.

I told my wife, Semolina, and my daughter, Mildred, "Larry said that policemen are squares."

"Oh, my!" said Semolina.

"He played bongos in the park at night. He says he is rebelling."

"Maybe he is going through a phase," Semolina said.

"Maybe," I said. "But he will be a bad influence on our daughter, Mildred."

"Larry is cool," Mildred said.

The next day Larry did his job. He is the lifeguard at the hotel swimming pool. Once, in Bayonne, New Jersey, he saved my life, and became my best friend. That is how I met Larry.

When he was finished working, he came to supper wearing a beret and sunglasses.

"Cool shades, Larry," Mildred said.

After supper, Larry read us a poem:

ARE MUFFINS LIKE FISH?
by Larry

fish are good to eat
and
    muffins
        are good too

I like
    them both
        muffins
    and
        fish
I like
    blueberry muffins
        but
        there
        are
        no
        blueberry
        fish.

The next night, Mildred had a beret too, and sunglasses.
She was dressed all in black.

After supper, Larry and Mildred played a tape of saxophone
music. They sat on the floor and snapped their fingers.

"That was crazy music," Larry said, when the tape was finished.

"Oh, I don't know," I said. "I thought it was pretty good."

Larry and Mildred looked at each other.

"He's square," Mildred said.

"He's got corners," Larry said.

"They think I am square," I said to Semolina.
"You are, you know," Semolina said. "You are not cool."
I looked in the mirror. "I am not square," I said. "I am cool."

That night, I heard Larry bongoing in the basement.

I went downstairs to the basement. Larry had turned out the lights. He had put a candle in a one-quart cod-liver-oil bottle. He was sitting and bongoing. Now and then he would stop bongoing, and take a sip of blueberry juice from a cup.

"Hey, Martin-man," Larry said. "I am digging my painting. You dig it too."

I dug his painting. It was a big painting, leaning against the wall. It looked like blobs.

"What is it a painting of?" I asked Larry.

"It is a whole bunch of crazy, far-out, never-ending, double-cool blueberry muffins," Larry said.

"It is very nice," I said. "Are the blue blobs the blueberries?"

"No, man. Those are the fish," Larry said.

"The fish?"

"Well, there are fish in it too."

"Cool," I said.

"You dig it?" Larry asked.

"I dig it the most," I said.

Two can play at this game, I thought.

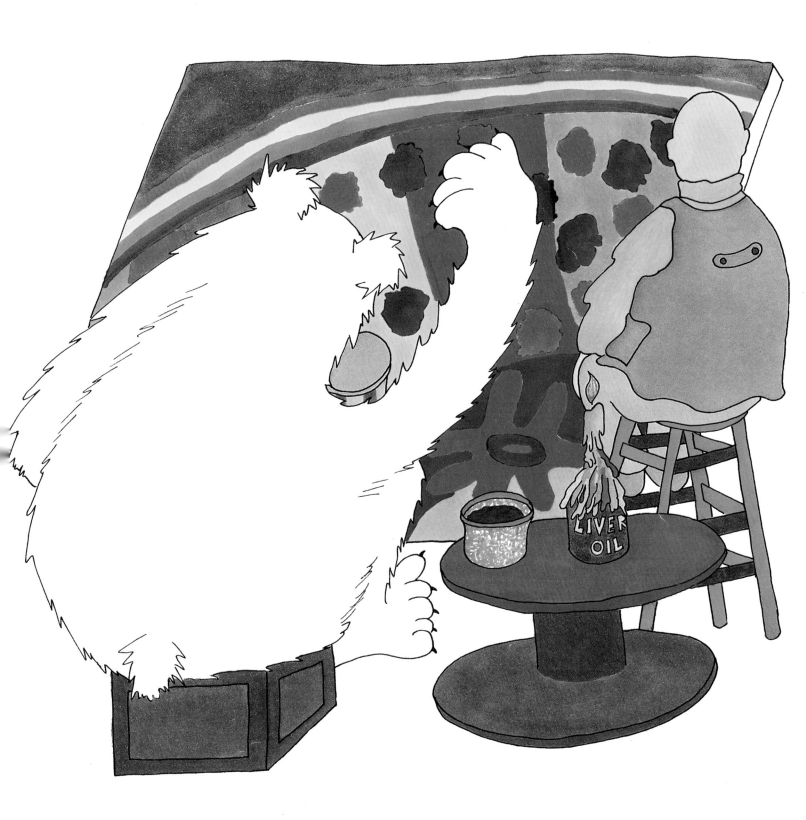

The next day, I got my black sweater. I got my shades. I got
my sandals. I went out and found a really nice pebble and hung
it around my neck on a leather shoelace. I looked in the mirror.
  "I am so cool," I said.

That night, at supper, I said, "After we finish our far-out fishcakes, let's all go out and make the scene. We'll dig some insane sounds, and some finger-popping poetry."

"Cool," Mildred said.

"Frantic," Larry said.

"I have to go upstairs and put on my cool clothes," Semolina said.

When Semolina came downstairs, she looked far-out.

"You are the coolest," I said.

"Those are crazy threads," Larry said.

"Mom, are your earrings lizards?" Mildred asked.

"They are plastic, dear," Semolina said. "Now let's go and have a groovy time."

Cafe MAMA·BEAR

We drove to the old part of town.

"Where are we going?" Larry asked.

"A place I know," I said. "Look! Here it is!"

"This is the Cafe Mama Bear!" Larry said. "I have always wanted to come here! It is the most!"

"To say the least," I said.

We went inside. The place was full of bears. There were beat bears, bent bears, banjo bears, bongo bears, buddy bears, baby bears, bald bears, barking bears, bawling bears, bearded bears, busy bears, barefoot bears and also honey bears, hairy bears, grizzly bears, growly bears, and bears of every description.

"Wow," Larry said. "Look at all the bears!"

"Hey! Larry Bear!" a bear said.

"Roy Bear!" Larry said. "Look! My brother is here!"

Bear Number One and Bear Number Three were there too.

They each held up two claws and said, "Peace, man."

We sat down at the table with Roy and Bear Number One, and Bear Number Three. A waitress bear brought us cups of hot blueberry juice.

Larry was excited. "This is the craziest!" he said.

"Shh!" Roy said. "In a minute Big Bear is going to lay some sweet sounds on us."

"Big Bear?" Larry asked. "Big Bear is here? Big Bear, the ever-loving, double-clutching, non-stop, groovy King of Cool is here? Right here?"

"Yep, brother bear," Roy said. "And there he is."

There was a little platform in the corner, and onto it stepped the biggest polar bear in the world.

"Cool cubs and cubbies, Big Bear loves you," Big Bear said.

All the bears snapped their claws to show they loved Big Bear too.

"Now Big Bear is going lay some sweet sounds on you, right from his big bear heart."

Snap snap snap snap snap, went the bears.

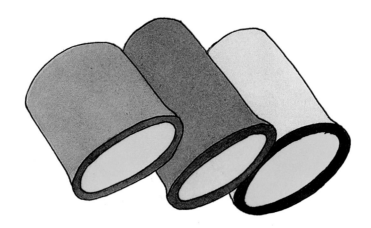

"But Big Bear needs a bongo cub to make frantic rhythms," Big Bear said. "And I understand that one of the great bongo bears of all time is with us tonight. So, come up here, Larry, you bongoing crazy-man."

"Me? He wants me? Big Bear wants me to play bongos?"

"Get up there, Larry," Roy said.

"Me?"

"Yes, you."

"Play bongos?"

"Right now."

"I'm going to faint."

"No, you're not."

"Play bongos for Big Bear?"

Snap snap snap snap snap.

Larry climbed up on the little stage. He sat on the little stool, and bent over his bongos. He raised one paw, and watched Big Bear. Big Bear nodded his head to Larry. Larry began to bongo, and Big Bear began to sing.

I am a big old polar bear
I come from where it's cold and wet
I am a big old polar bear
I come from where it's cold and wet
If they had pizza where I come from
I'd be living up there yet

Larry bongoed softly when Big Bear sang the words, and bongoed loudly in between the words.

The bears snapped their claws.

I am a great big polar bear
I like to sleep out on the ice
I am a great big polar bear
I like to sleep out on the ice
Roll in the water, catch yourself a fish
Mmmm, mmmm, there's nothing quite so nice

Larry did some fast bongoing at the end of this one. The bears liked it.

I like to float near the bottom
And I like to float on top
I like to float near the bottom of the water
Yes, and I like to float on top
I like to bob up and down
Oh yes, like I'm never going to stop

Then Larry joined in, and sang with Big Bear.

Give this bear a muffin
And he will always be your friend
Listen to me
Give this bear a great big blueberry muffin
And he will always be your very best friend
Just hand over that muffin, Mama
And I will love you to the very end

Big Bear gave Larry a big bear-hug, and all the bears snapped their claws.
"Big Bear! Larry Bear!" they shouted.

Then Larry put on his beret, and we all walked to the car.
Larry smiled quietly all the way back to the hotel.

"Did you have a nice time at the Cafe Mama Bear?" I asked Larry.

"It was cool," Larry said.

To each other,
D. P. and J. P.

Text copyright © 1998 by Daniel Pinkwater
Illustrations copyright © 1998 by Jill Pinkwater
All rights reserved
Marshall Cavendish, 99 White Plains Road, Tarrytown, New York 10591
The text of this book is set in 16 point Esprit Book
The illustrations are rendered in pen and ink and colored markers
Printed in Italy
First edition
1   3   5   6   4   2

Library of Congress Cataloging-in-Publication Data. Pinkwater, Daniel Manus, date.
Bongo Larry / Daniel Pinkwater ; illustrated by Jill Pinkwater.   p.   cm. Summary: Larry the
polar bear's new interest in playing the bongos leads to an impromptu performance with
Big Bear at the Cafe Mama Bear. ISBN 0-7614-5020-3 (reinforced bdg.)
[1. Polar bear—Fiction. 2. Bears—Fiction. 3. Musicians—Fiction. 4.Humorous stories.]
I. Pinkwater, Jill, ill. II. Title.
PZ7.P6335Bnf   1998   [E]—dc21   97-3451   CIP   AC